Young Learner's

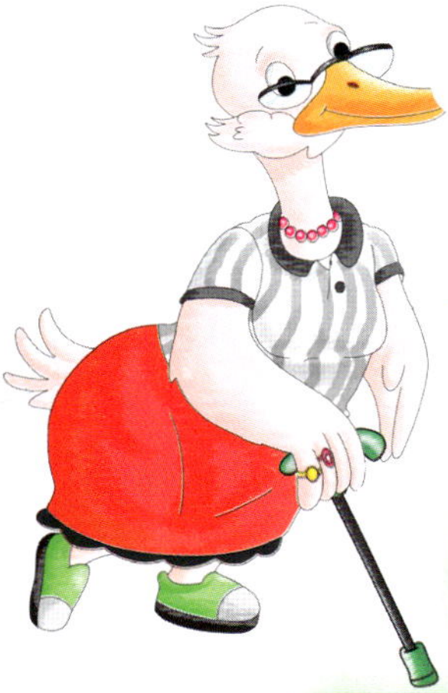

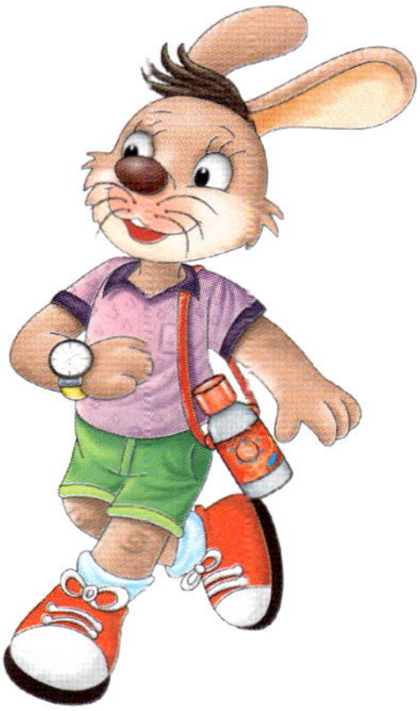

Buds Helps Mrs. Dory

Sangita Koushik

Buds the rabbit loved to go for long walks on the sandy beach every day.

The sea and the beach looked beautiful.
Cool and fresh winds blew all the time.

Every day while walking, Buds would pass by a sweet old lady with a walking stick.

They would exchange smiles as they walked past each other. Buds admired her for never missing her walks.

One fine morning as he saw her, Buds decided to talk to the old lady. He greeted her politely and said, "I am Buds." The old lady replied, "Hello Buds! I am Mrs. Dory."

Buds said, "Mrs. Dory, I admire that you never miss your walks." Mrs. Dory smiled and replied, "Thank you child! I have noticed that you never miss your walks either!"

They talked some more and then Buds took leave of Mrs. Dory and walked on. After a while, he decided to go back.

As he walked, he thought, "Hmm! I wonder where is Mrs. Dory. I should have crossed her by now."

Buds walked a little further and then he saw Mrs. Dory. He was shocked for she was lying on the ground.

She had fainted! Quickly, Buds opened his water bottle and sprinkled some water on her face.

Mrs. Dory opened her eyes. But she was too weak to walk or talk. Buds decided to get help.

But first, he helped her sit up against a tree and gave her some water to drink. Then, he ran to get help.

Luckily, he had to run only for a short distance before he came across a car. He waved it down and asked the driver for help.

Together they rushed to the place where Buds had left Mrs. Dory. They helped her into the car and took her to a hospital nearby.

The doctor at the hospital gave her some medicines. Then, Buds took her to her house. Mrs. Dory thanked him for his timely help. They became good friends. They also became walking buddies!

Moral: Always help someone in need.

Printed in India